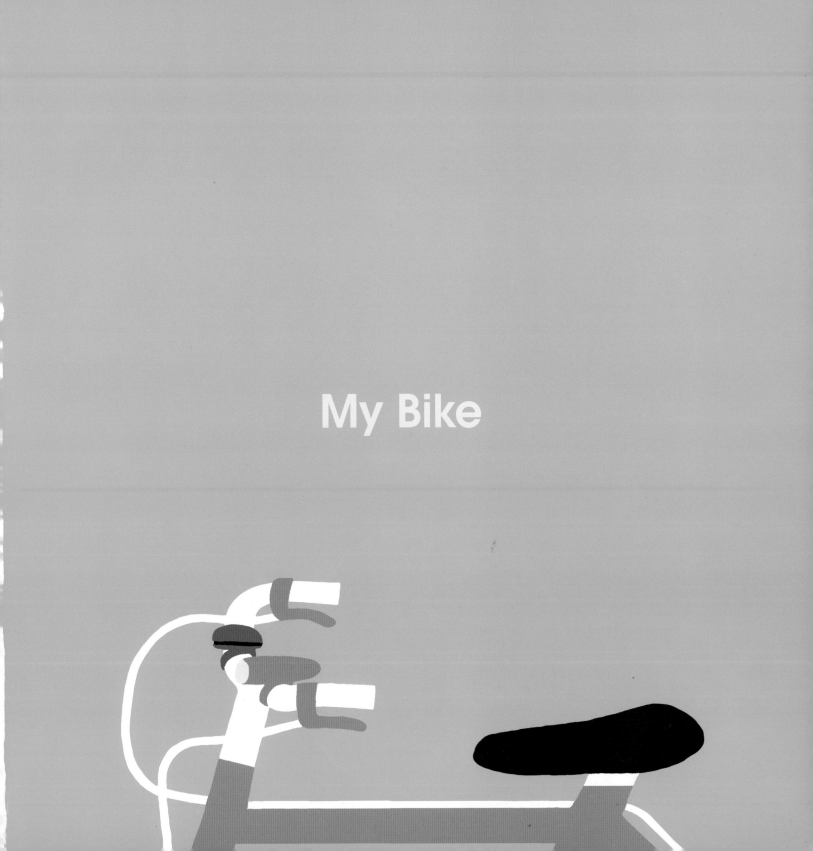

My Bike

My Bike

illustrated by

Byron Barton

 **Greenwillow Books,** *An Imprint of HarperCollins Publishers*

My Bike. Copyright © 2015 by Byron Barton. All rights reserved. Manufactured in China.
For information address HarperCollins Children's Books,
a division of HarperCollins Publishers, 195 Broadway, New York, NY 10007.
www.harpercollinschildrens.com

The full-color art was created in Adobe Photoshop™. The text type is ITC Avant Garde Gothic.

Library of Congress Cataloging-in-Publication Data
Barton, Byron.
My bike / Byron Barton.
pages cm
"Greenwillow Books."
Summary: Tom tells all about his bicycle, his ride to work past trucks, cars,
and even elephants, and his work as a circus performer.
ISBN 978-0-06-233699-6 (trade ed.)
[1. Bicycles and bicycling—Fiction. 2. Circus—Fiction.] I. Title.
PZ7.B2848Mv 2015 [E]—dc23 2014013919
First Edition
15 16 17 SCP 10 9 8 7 6 5 4 3 2 1

Greenwillow Books

To Susan Hirschman,
lover of children's books
and responsible for the making of
many, many books for children,
including this one

I am Tom.

This is my bicycle.

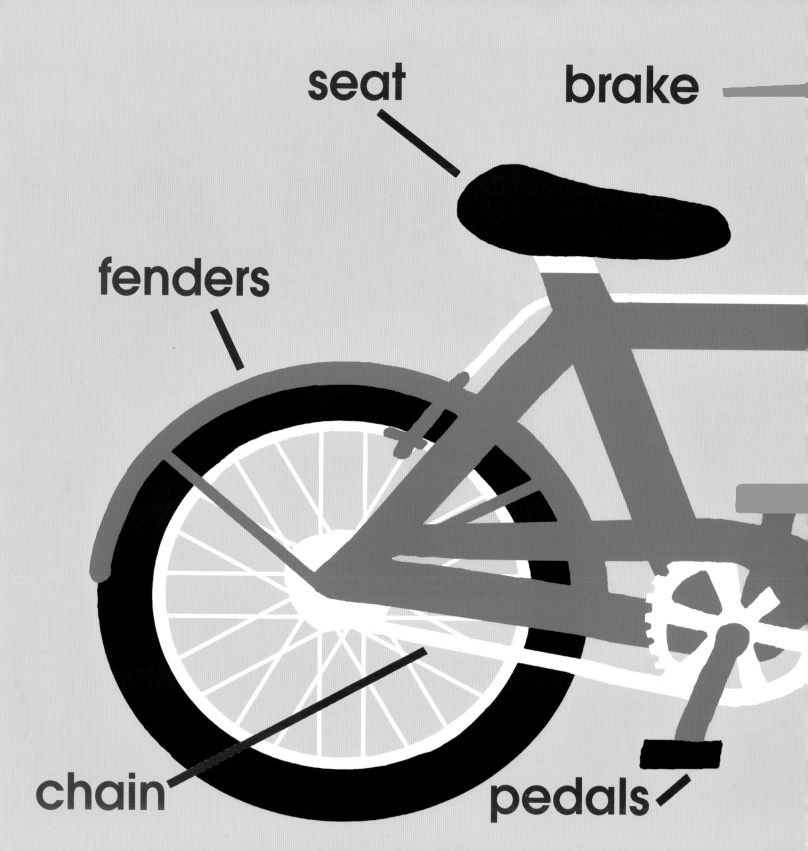

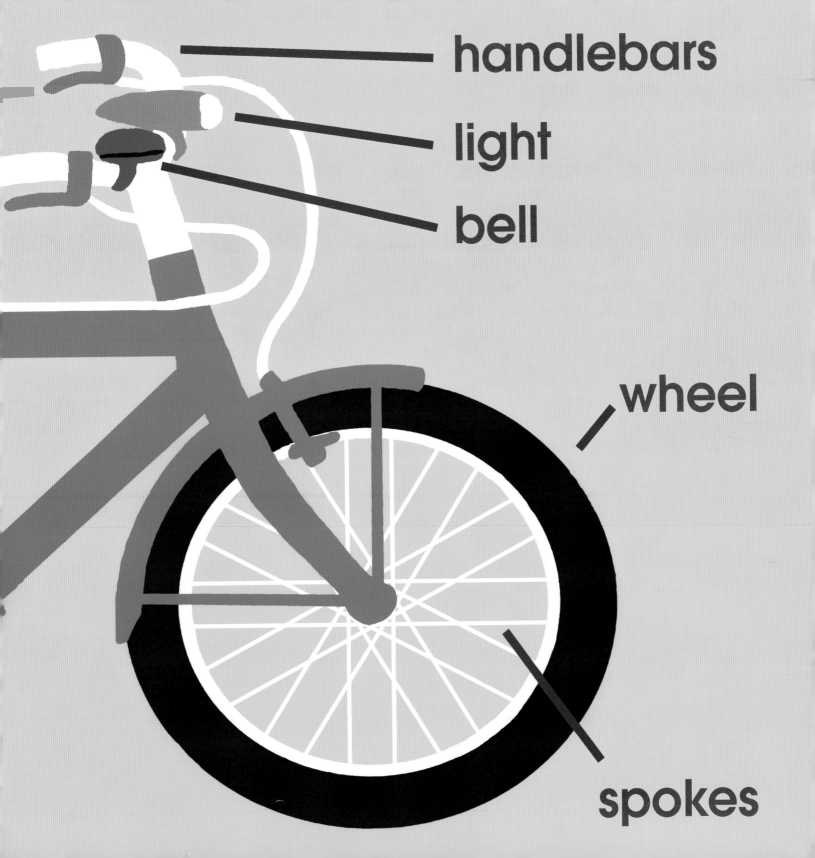

handlebars

light

bell

wheel

spokes

helmet

backpack

I ride
my bicycle
to work.

On the way,

I pass trucks

and lots of cars

ONE WAY

and lots of people

and monkeys

and acrobats

and tigers

and lions

and elephants.

When I get there,
I park my bicycle.

I put on my uniform.

I put on my makeup.

I climb
a tall ladder

and I go to work

on my unicycle.

Look!
No hands!